Small Moods

•

SHANE KOWALSKI

Future Tense Books

Portland, Oregon

Some stories appeared previously in: *Bad Nudes, Bathhouse Journal,
Blue Arrangements' Lazy Susan, Electric Literature's The Commuter,
Forever Magazine, Funhouse Magazine, Guesthouse, Jellyfish Review,
Meetinghouse, Milk Candy Review, New Delta Review, New World
Writing, Nightblock, Ohio Edit, Passages North, Peach Mag, The
Southampton Review, Tammy, Wildness, X-RAY*, and the chapbooks
Dog Understander (Frontier Slumber, 2017) and *How I Solve How I
Feel* (Ghost City Press, 2020).

Paperback ISBN: 978-1-892061-90-4

Edited by Kevin Sampsell and Emma Alden.
Layout by Michael Kazepis.
Cover design by Michael J. Seidlinger

First edition. Printed in the United States of America.

Published by Future Tense Books.
www.futuretensebooks.com
Portland, Oregon

A Good Start

The day I was born, I came out vomiting. The doctor looked at me vomiting in his gloved hands and started vomiting. The nurses, one had a mole on her face that was admirable, started vomiting. My father, readying the scissors to cut the cord, started vomiting. My mother, seeing my father vomiting and admiring him to a sick degree, started vomiting. I remember, because I have a very good memory, that I saw everyone else around me vomiting in the delivery room, and because it revolts me, as most things do, when people try and emulate me, I stopped vomiting.

Another Day

A man walking his dog down your street turns out to be Gertrude Stein. She is pleasant and carries with her a drizzly cloud of Midwestern charm. She keeps saying things like 'Moaning keeps the snake apart' and 'Stacking a lack comes to a past.' It's like a chant that is trying to get you into bed. Her dog is not a dog.

It's been vexing, these days: nothing is the thing we keep looking for, even as we continue accumulating facts.

The Beating Heart, The Silver Platter, The Best Path

They led me into the forest where they sat me on a stump and told me to eat the heart that had been prepared for me on a silver platter. The heart pumped in and out as if it were still a part of something alive. Even I had to admit it looked very aesthetically pleasing on the silver platter. It was the ideal example of what one would have thought of when thinking of "beating heart on silver platter." I wanted to ask questions but for one reason or another I did not. It was a "no asking questions" mood. Later on, when I had the time to reflect on the whole affair, I thought of the questions I would've asked had I the mood to: *Why have you led me here? Who are you? Why are you asking me to eat this beating heart on a silver platter?* The forest chattered with the cicadas that had recently awakened after seventeen years of being underground. The sound was deafening. The ideal example of "deafening sound." Threads of sunlight unspooled from the canopies of dense branches above. I thought: If not for this very strange circumstance, I would be enjoying the pleasant and quiet mysticism of this forest. When the moment finally came, I wouldn't call giving in to their demands and eating the beating heart a submission, but it was a cautioning. I think it comes from childhood, when I thought the worst part of being loved was when I was still loved despite my resistance, my disobedience. So, I cautioned always on the side of obedience, of order. Now that I'm dead, I ponder in perpetual and unwavering darkness if this was always the best path to lead a life down.

Reliability

Being back in my hometown has been pleasant enough. Some things leave you and some things you feel selfish for having not kept. For instance, I had forgotten about Mr. Palomer and his daughter, who keep dying and coming back. They die in the evening. Then in the morning, they'll be back to life. Look in on them and they'll be eating their khaki oatmeal together as the birds chirp on the red roofs. It's quite unremarkable when you think about how reliable the narrative of their dying and coming back to life really is. It is easy to forget reliable things.

In any case, I'm more interested in the case of the girl who has begun to lie down naked in the sand of Lake Wixxcip. She lies face down and the sun has browned her bottom and the backs of her thighs and shoulders. She refuses to get up when you call on her. She will get up when she's through, whenever she determines that is. Then she'll return again, facedown in the sand, whenever she feels like it.

Whenever she *feels like it?*

There's no reason for her to be doing this. It's fascinating. I'm fascinated when somebody is controlled by how they feel.

Dreaming Dog

Her name was Wendy and she was a lawyer—
or training to be a lawyer?—and we were in bed
together. She wanted to know if I had named my
dog after Martin Luther King Jr. or Martin Luther.

Who? I said.

Your dog's name is Martin Luther? she said.

Yeah, I said.

So it has to be one, she said. She was getting
very fervent with me and I felt guilty.

We were just lying in bed after a good time
filled with a lot of touching and I had practically
forgotten about Martin Luther. When she first
asked me about his name, I almost said, *What dog?*

She looked at me. I looked at her, trying to feel
her out. Then I looked at Martin Luther, who was
sleeping in the corner.

Does it make a difference? I said.

Kind of? she said. Yes.

I told her I didn't name him. Which was the
truth. I got him from a shelter, and miraculously at

that, since I had no prospects at the time and I was living in an apartment in that terrible small city that was like a closed hand. I had the sense the shelter just wanted to dump him on someone—wash their hands of him. He was an old dog, with a wobbling walk, and he seemed to have a canine form of Tourette's. He'd howl depressively at nothing or anything during the day. It would wear him out by the evening and he'd sleep like a dead dog through the night. I considered changing his name when I got him, to kind of, you know, make him my own. But then thought: How rude would that be? After nine years, what kind of a jerk changes the sound a dog knows himself by? Who even was I to name something?

What would you have named him, if you did? Wendy said.

You ask hard questions, I told Wendy.

Then I puffed up my pillow and let my big head slowly sink back into it. Wendy, thinking of her next question, watched me do this.

In the corner the dog was fast asleep. He snored and his one good paw moved now and then. He was dreaming now. He had just been barking it seemed, and watching us on the bed, but now he was dreaming of dancing tennis balls in hula skirts, of cars that slowed down and talked in baby voices, of gods with hands used only for petting.

A Mood

Someone is always ruining my anger.

Flattening it out into the dirt.

In spring it pops out of the soil like fresh tenderness.

Someone comes and snips a bud and puts it in their hair.

And it rains and rains all day on Saturday.

*The Butterfly's Wing, The Secret Word, The Tiny
Little Deranged Monkey*

We are in the moment of the butterfly's wing
silently flapping miles away...

What secret word will we use to recognize each
other after this unnoticed moment passes?

The horizon ends long before we think it does...

A disintegrated shadow on the sidewalk wearing
a pearl necklace is the only clue...

I had a dream a tiny little deranged monkey
on a unicycle was wheeling itself around in the
middle of deserted downtown, and in the dream
I looked at this tiny little deranged monkey and
thought, *Love*...

I am Not a Little Teapot

I wasn't good at being a child. My name was Bill.

When "I'm A Little Teapot" would play, I would think: I am not a little teapot.

I could physically sense this in my body. The impossibility of things.

When other children would sing, I'd think they were liars. I couldn't trust them. Or worse, I *could* trust them—which meant I was trapped in a world filled with teapots. And so I kept my distance for years, leery of the scalding contents inside them all...

Jewels

The day Jesus died, a stray dog snuck into Herod's palace and ate three of his jewels.

The dog then crossed the deserts, not once stopping to partake in the mirages of water that beckoned here and there.

It arrived in the city of Cairo during a plague of locusts...

The dog drank from a bowl of priest's blood and didn't die...

A woman who wore bells around her ankles knelt down and petted the dog...

I think you know where I am going with this story...

Obviously, that dog...he was my father's father's father's father...

"The Country"

My friend, whom I won't name because she was an enemy of the state, lived very far away, and not by choice. Every month I made the trip to where she lived in "the country." I brought her another month's supply of bread when I went. That is the thing she missed most living where she lived, she'd say. The bread. I was happy to make the long and sometimes fretful trip to where she lived in "the country" to give her bread. I enjoyed her company. Sometimes something situationy would happen between us, which was exciting.

Last time I saw her she said she didn't mind living the way she lived. She held a dark loaf of bread in her hands and squeezed it, then remarked that she might get a dog out here.

I don't remember the last words I said to her. I often wonder what they were but I know they won't mean anything now.

Next time I visited her, the house where she lived in "the country" had been ransacked, half-burned, spotted with rusty-red stains. It wasn't doing a very good job of covering up whatever had taken place there. It was as if something very personal had happened.

It's probably best I stop talking about it now.

You See

I was brought up in a cult. The religion had
something to do with blood and lambs. I was in
love with Sue-Ellen. In the back of the pickup truck
with my hair going wild. Dark summer days when
we'd hide in the woods. Do voices. Feel like music
was being played in the air and only we could hear
it. Being too nervous to eat your dinner at the table.
Wavering, watery tension filling up the kitchen. The
one light overhead that shed light on nothing. No
neighbor would come. Tried hiding my underwear
under the bed. Pushed all my books into the closet.
Cried because it felt like the only thing I could
control. Could turn it off and on, like a television.
God, or what, help me. One thunderstormed night
I shriveled up in bed and wouldn't dare look at the
window looking at me. You see. All my life felt like
eyes looking in from a dark night at me. I'm with
you, in your cities, in your dreams, I mourn for
something just like you. Do you hear me? I haven't
said a word.

All-Time Bestseller

I wrote a book. It sold for a billion dollars. I bought an alligator on a gold leash. I paid to shoot a stockbroker in the head just for the ethics of it. I bought a bank and set it on fire. Somebody who had read my book came up to me in the middle of it and said, Wow, can I have an autograph? I autographed their book with "Oh Well." One day I paid a man to recreate the undignified mental decline of ronald reagan in painful, pitiless detail. I bought a pair of $1,000-dollar high heels just to lick them. Eventually it was time to write another book. But what can one write when one has already tasted the fruits of fantasy's labor?

Unemployed

Someone asks you to do something about your past.

What can you do? You're just a rapper with five hundred gold chains sans pants.

I have been sleeping but not sleeping for six years. I have ruined my life in the name of space exploration and fine dining.

I am so bored with what I'm saying I almost feel accomplished!

Look at these personality chops I have. Doesn't it make you want to take a ride in my hooptie? I have six-thousand-year-old champagne we can pour on each other's genitals.

I like when people call me Uncle.

I want a zoo filled with empty cages…

Who Invented Xmas Music

I wanted him to make me do things. He was three hundred miles away and I'd stare into the little face of my phone, waiting for my next order. He was mostly very unimaginative with his orders. He'd make me clean the bathroom nude (he always used the word *nude*) or mop the kitchen floor nude or put clothespins on my nipples nude. He'd send me a message from three hundred miles away during my day at work to remove my underwear and stick it in my bra. He called my underwear panties, and at first it was quite nice being infantilized like that but quickly I lost the plot when it didn't go anywhere new. Still, I'd remove my panties anyway in the tiny little bathroom where I worked and take a pic of them stuffed in my bra and send it to him. Not doing it would feel worse, was my opinion then. Even if they were bad rules I wanted to obey them. I enjoyed him telling me what to do from that far away, no matter how uncreative he was. If he was right there, in person, I'd be so bored out of my mind I'd become dangerous. If I had been a mother then and forced to be in the same room with that dull man, I'd drown my beautiful children in a bathtub to save them the boredom of this man. Him being that far away and ordering me to do things was what made it erotic and exciting—I was really doing it myself! It was only by that math I felt calm and natural in my body. He'd often say he could drive down or I could drive up and we'd have some "fun," but all I'd do was shudder like a bat in daylight at the idea.

I liked being told to stand in the corner naked, hands on my head, while he monitored me from the little screen on my phone. I liked taking orders from a man so small I could turn him off with a push of a button, but still I didn't. I liked being told to put on my dog collar I bought from PetPlus and drink water out of a bowl on the floor. But I hated the thought of him right there, next to me, body to body, being so… who he was. I knew what I wanted, could summon it if I wanted it, and could dismiss it just as easily. Which is why he stayed so far away. Which is what allowed me to follow his orders.

I'm a long way away from that man now but the distance has created a kind of clarity. The kind you believe despite hard evidence. Which makes me think of my father and how he must have felt when he told my sister and I that he was the man who invented Xmas music. He'd pronounce the X. He came here from a distant country. Met and married my mother here. My sister and I were born here after. When we were little and that sweet Xmas music filled the air with its directives to be jolly, imploring us to dance happily, Father would tell my dancing sister and me in his clumsy English that it was he who made this beautiful music. He was the man who invented the idea of music that communicated the wondrous Xmas spirit! We'd stare with our big dark eyes at him telling us his merry tale of self-invention, which we took as absolute fact.

He had traveled many miles from the place he was born, a land where he had felt afraid and small a lot of the time, to feel how he wanted to feel.

Every time I hear that music now there is always a fiasco in my heart. As if those two trains in that math problem in school are traveling great distances to collide with each other inside me.

I remember trying to convince the other children in school how great a man my father was. My chest swelling when telling them.

Why's your dad so great? they'd ask, their faces unbelieving, on the verge of bullying.

I didn't care. I was a believer. With my arms above my head in astonishment I said: He invented Xmas music!

The Object

Sometimes I love to hate a thing loved by a person I hate.

Sometimes even more than loving a thing I love, or even loving a thing someone I love loves. Sometimes it isn't even sometimes. It is all times.

All times?!

So much time I've spent with my attention elsewhere that, at this point, it can't be called elsewhere anymore. It's here, always, in front of me: the object of my "affection."

A Humid Fugue

A person outside is waiting for you to react to your life.

They keep checking their wrist like a watch.

Suddenly it's summer. The leaves are erect. Animals crawl out of the forest to take our jobs.

Then: push back, of course. A fervor. A national sentiment suddenly happens. Committees are made. Groups are formed. Petitions are marched about. Rallies are festooned. Legislation festers. A humid fugue falls over it all like a wool blanket.

Abrupt attention is paid to the flag.

We always want the thing we never wanted when it's finally being taken from us.

How do we stop ourselves from stopping ourselves from being gentle?

NSFW

Something doesn't make sense about this man. His facial features, his hands, the way he speaks, his tail.

It's because he's a squirrel!

These are strange days when we can mistake a squirrel for a man. It is best if we just go back to work, ignore it. The manager will fire us if we don't.

Still Thought Having

It could be not true but I'm pretty sure my family had a plant with a face that could sing when I was young.

There was a movie about a magic car with no driver that would let young lovers choke each other inside of it.

Yes, I had a teacher, too, who told us that all weather could be explained by God's disgusting body. Rain was sweat, snow was dandruff, fog was bad breath, the warm sun was pee.

Of course there was a dog. It died playing with a stick. The stick was a stick of dynamite.

Someone kept calling the house and hanging up. I think it was the Ghost of Future Sex.

A dream I had: I think it was trying to tell me something, anything. It spoke as if it had been a painting for ages and only now, free from the bonds of its brushstrokes, could it speak. Imagine that: being stuck on a wall forever, only being able to use your eyes.

Eyes aren't everything. Eyes can be a curse.

I Bought An Octopus

I bought an octopus instead of a puppy.

I don't know…

The woman at the pet store said an octopus comes with very low responsibility.

They are their own pets.

I wasn't quite sure what that meant.

But goddamn it…

The children were kind of disappointed, but I could tell they were also interested in the octopus.

They stared at it in its big tank that was very expensive. They started to really like it, I think. The octopus.

As a family we stared at the octopus in its tank. I felt great. Like I did something really good for the family. It was a very warm kind of feeling.

The children smiled at the octopus.

The octopus squished itself into one of the corners of the tank, behind a decorative piece of coral. I don't know about coral but I thought it was pretty. All the way home, I thought about the coral and not about the octopus.

I smiled at my wife and my wife slightly smiled back at me.

It's safe, right? she said.

Of course! I said. They're their own pets…

She said, What does that mean?

I said it's safe and not a lot of responsibility.

Though I wasn't really sure if it was safe and that maybe the responsibility would be too much.

I said of course again so she would acquiesce to "believe" me.

Later, while the children played with the octopus, I did some research online.

I discovered octopi were very smart and could even climb out of their own tanks.

"If not for the need of water, they could potentially be our overlords," said one website that was purple-colored.

I started to think maybe I had made a bad choice…

Had I put my family in danger?

My forehead—it was wet.

I told the children it was time for bed.

But Dadddddddddd, they said.

No buts, I said. The octopus will be there tomorrow.

Ohhh okayyyyy, they said and went upstairs and pretended to brush their teeth.

I checked the tank. The octopus was still behind the decorative coral in the tank. It had not moved.

I smiled.

I worried too much.

We all went to sleep.

That night, I had a dream that the octopus climbed out of its tank, bound my wife with six of its arms, and then with the other two arms made love to my wife.

After it was done with her, it went for the children…

Then I woke up.

I went downstairs and checked the expensive tank.

The octopus was still there.

I stared at it and it stared at me.

In the dark.

That's really messed up, said my wife in the morning after I told her my dream.

Having senses of humor, we both chuckled at this strange dream.

Uncomfortably.

Sipping coffee.

Was it so strange?

I wondered.

Had I put my family in danger?

Just to be sure, I got rid of the octopus later that day.

The woman at the pet store shrugged and said something that pretty much meant octopi are not for everyone.

I handed over the octopus. I handed over the tank.

I kept the decorative coral.

I don't know. Some things are worth it.

Driving home, a song of optimistic yelling came on the radio and I took it as a sign I had done the right thing.

I would tell the children the octopus died.

That would be the easy thing to do.

So they wouldn't know I was a fucking coward.

Irresponsible fucking coward.

I shook my head at myself while parked at a red light, exorcising myself of the deep blue shame inside me.

I touched the coral and somehow communicated my anxiety into it and it shimmered.

I drove home.

The children were sad.

I gave them ice cream cones.

But how did it die? said one of them.

I shrugged my shoulders. I had failed to think up a good death for the octopus.

Goddamn…

Fucking loser…

It got very old, I said.

I explained to them that maybe we could eventually get a puppy one day.

Ohhh okayyyyy, they said. They stood there licking the ice cream cones down to nothing.

Later we all went to sleep.

And after a while I woke up in the dead of night.

I could hear the soft hum of ocean.

I went downstairs.

Looked at the empty spot where the tank had been.

My wife put a vase with old, soon-to-go flowers there.

I stared at the vase of flowers.

The vase of flowers "stared" back.

The possible worlds we get to live in are out there…

The problem is we get to choose…

The Mail

Having sex with the mailman doesn't get you your mail faster, is what Mother used to tell us.

That was her advice to us growing up.

We were not sure what she meant.

We had sex with the mailman anyway.

All of us, one by one, as we got older.

His name was Dale.

We didn't know much about him, other than his sexual practices and tics. We kind of built a story up in our heads, each of us independently, that he was a secretly happy man. Sure, he was morose yet steady in coitus, but we imagined him being a very vigorous man outside of the bedroom. Well-dressed and well-coiffed. Ready for bright and distant lands like Vegas. Holding the nyloned legs of pretty girls in his bejeweled fingers.

Mother and Pop were not comfortable with the culture, and were always very sacred when it came to people conducting their business. People at work were to be treated with a holiness and reverence. Having sex with them was blasphemous.

So we decided to not call it having sex.

It was our little secret phrase between us.

We called it getting the mail.

Grief

She was an affectless girl who grew her boyfriend from a dollop of whale's blubber. Her original boyfriend had drowned in Xxxilixp Lake. She was always better in the water than him. Instead of feeling sad, she took the blubber and rubbed it on her genitals. She rubbed it until the blubber grew and reshaped itself and became her boyfriend. He was softer, tenderer, less juvenile. She could rub him against her genitals and he wouldn't tire. She brought him home to meet her parents, who long ago had died and were now blubber parents. She petted Bingo, her beloved dog, slobbery, also made of blubber, while her blubber parents asked her blubber boyfriend what his parents did for a living.

Relief

The man and woman believe their house to be haunted. The man and woman are not married or romantically involved. They just live together.

The house they live in produces photos out of nowhere. The walls sprout frames, people inside the frames; the people are vaguely recognizable, but only very vaguely.

Neither the man nor the woman is superstitious. They believe in the haunting of their house but that doesn't mean they believe it really means anything more than that. They know some things, on occasion, turn into other things.

They collect all the spontaneously sprouted photos and burn them in the fire pit out back. They listen to the people in them scream. Some of them in agony, some of them in the faintest relief possible at having averted another possible future...

Why I Love The Hand Lady

Please, let me tell you about my sexual exploits. It won't take long!

I am very in love with people who seem to always be at home. I am! I like how you never see them on the street.

Hey, is there a dog in your life right now?

Sure hope so!

Hey, has anyone ever given you their hand as a gift?

I knew a woman once who had so many hands, she was called the Hand Lady. You could walk in and out of her home and feel like you were being waved at. What a lovely feeling. I love that woman. I love how she collected hands, keeping them tidy but never offering her own.

Buyer Beware

We bought a house. That house had a little house in it. Not just little. Very, extremely tiny. Not even fit for a mouse or its children. Insects maybe. It was a mystery. It was in the Victorian Gothic style. We looked at it, walked around it, making sure not to crush it completely from existence. We had not noticed this tinier house when we were buying the larger house. Who built this house? we wondered. From out of the new-home silence came a voice— It was I! said the voice. Ignacio! The Architect of All Tiny Things!

Naturally

There is another dimension where everything is naturally heart shaped. The shape of the heart does not have the effect it has in our dimension.

Shapes we think of as "normal" in our dimension seem alien and original in that dimension.

Round pizzas, for instance, look quite strange and thrilling there.

When it is time to bury their loved ones, the people of that other dimension fit them into heart shaped coffins. Which, of course, to them, is very tasteful.

The Magic Orgasm

A peasant boy, leading his family's dairy cow back from grazing, came across a troll who offered him a trade. For your cow, dear boy, I will offer you an orgasm, said the troll.

The peasant boy looked at the troll. That doesn't seem like a fair trade, said the peasant boy.

Ah! said the troll. This is no ordinary orgasm though. This is a magic orgasm! Here, see for yourself!

The troll held it out in his hand, the size of a bean, green and glowing.

This is my family's only cow, said the peasant boy. If I trade it to you for this magic orgasm, what will I tell my family? They are poor and their spirits are low. This cow is our only source of what little income we have.

You may share this magic orgasm with your family, said the troll. It is really best to share.

You're saying this magic orgasm will provide us with income? asked the peasant boy.

It will provide you with more than income, said the troll.

More than income?! said the peasant boy.

The troll held the magic orgasm out to the boy. Do we have a trade? the troll asked.

After giving it one last thought, the peasant boy agreed.

When he arrived home later without the cow, his family berated him: What do you mean you traded Katinka? And for a bean?

But this is no bean, said the peasant boy. This is a magic orgasm!

The peasant boy's mother walked over and slapped him on both cheeks. The peasant boy's father took the magic orgasm from the boy's hand and threw it to the ground. Both his mother and father took turns stepping on it. They invited his twelve siblings to come and step on it. They stomped and mashed it as the peasant boy watched.

What a stupid son we've made! his mother and father lamented. They walked away.

The peasant boy fell to his knees. A feeling was overtaking him. It seemed like it would never finish, never die. His cheeks, red and warm, felt like two apples: if bitten, they might curse someone with eternal relief.

No Change Here

When someone says "change" I think they are saying "Shane." Even if I know very clearly and contextually that what they are saying is "change," I will hear "Shane."

...Be the "Shane" you want to see in the world...

...A "Shane" is gonna come...

When people call me on the phone I'll usually say, Sorry but "Change" isn't here, and I hang up.

The Fat Suit My Dead Mother Lived In

She was living in a large suit designed to replicate the sensation of being fat. I found out after she died.

Her apartment was where the universe came to be small. Everything in it was tiny. If I were small, I would think my dead mother's apartment was very normal, maybe perfect.

I'm abnormally tall for a woman. The last man I went on a date with kept calling me How's The Weather Up There and asking to see my feet.

At first I thought everything just felt smaller because I was so much bigger, but that's not the case. The couch was small, the bed was small, the still-on television was small, the refrigerator was small. I wondered why nobody turned the television off. I found it comforting.

Everything was so small it was almost hard to see the suit on the floor next to the bed. Even though the suit was so large, the vast smallness of everything else in her apartment made me blind to largeness.

I discovered that largeness in a world of smallness, like my dead mother's apartment, was just the absence of smallness. A blank, negative space that held limitless and mysterious possibilities.

Then from my great height, at a certain angle, like looking into those puzzles you have to blur your eyes to understand, the suit came into focus.

It was pinkish pale, as if performing as the skin of a white person who collected cute knick knacks and would insist on finishing a stale pot of coffee. Where there should have been a head was a hole where the skin stopped. My mother put her head through that absence of skin, I thought sentimentally.

On the large fat suit were very small appendages on the chest and a very small, almost unnoticeable, appendage between the legs.

Sniffing it, the suit smelled like something I imagined my mother smelled like on certain days of the year, in midsummer, when everyone's just waiting for something more to happen but it doesn't. It just doesn't.

Both of us kept our baffling conundrums to ourselves while she was alive. No amount of profound certainty could help.

Something about the situation called me to enter the suit. It was a little small for me and tight, so I had to strip and then curl inside the suit, crunch myself smaller. When I was in, I walked around in my dead mother's apartment. I wanted to lie down in her bed but to get to the bedroom I had to curl myself even tighter. It seemed the doorways were smaller now that I was in the suit. Instead of lying on a bed in the fat suit, it felt like I was lying on my dead mother. I squeezed my head through the hole where the skin stopped. The motion of doing that—of squeezing my head through—summoned the unfurnitured house of my childhood…

Between the ages of nine and thirteen I had a series of nightmares there. I was constantly being chased through maze-like hallways by what I called The Fat Man. Each morning, I would cry and tell mother about it. She said don't worry. She placed a small hand over my already large forehead. She was an incredibly comforting mother when forced to be. She told me The Fat Man was harmless. She said: The Fat Man loves you very much.

Try And Stop Me

I can't even afford to talk, but I still do. I pet a lamb soaked in blood in the pouring rain.

I was put on this earth to make those with money miserable. I screamed out of a window once that I was pregnant even though I wasn't and can never be pregnant.

Try and stop me.

I am like a tiny baby geisha that will keep you up all night.

I am like a dollar bill in the shape of a swan on fire.

Do you hear that steely skronking? It's the saxophone that will score your death.

I am coming for you and you don't even know it. Because how could you? You're not even reading this…

The Exact Shape of Hawaii!

A young man knocks on her door one day after she has fallen into a deep nap and says he is her long lost son.

No you're not, she says. My son has been missing for fifteen years.

Look at the birthmark, he says and shows her the birthmark.

She gasps when she sees the birthmark—the same as her long lost son's birthmark—the exact shape of Hawaii!

She says come in and he comes in and she fills him in on the life he's missed for the last fifteen years: his brother's marriage (*very wonderful rose-gold candlesticks*), the death of Grinch (*good old pup*), the death of his own father (*zapped by a malfunctioning outlet*), etc.

He sits there and receives it all. Wow, he says.

Wait until your brother sees you, she says. This is a miracle. Our family is coming back together.

She sleeps dreadfully that night. She thinks of all the times, when her youngest son first went missing, that she had the thought that it was the wrong son who went missing. She would say it out loud. Her husband would scold her when she said it out loud while lying in bed waiting for sleep to snip the dead bloom of day away. She didn't feel guilt then, in the moment, and perhaps even said it to receive the scolding, but she had felt guilt ever since. It felt like drinking a cold glass of water after being thirsty for many days. Now that he's back, it is a chance to begin fresh, she thinks. She goes and listens in on him while he sleeps in his old room: noiseless, neutral, home.

The next day the brothers are reunited. So you're really him? the older brother says.

I missed you, brother, says the young man.

But the brother is suspicious. He asks to see the birthmark and nods when he sees it. He hugs his long lost brother as if he's hugging a shape of something that is smoldering. We'll throw a party as a homecoming, the mother says, wrapping around her boys like lasso.

Later, when it's dark and everyone in the world that he knows is sleeping, the older brother begins to think. For fifteen years he has known only one kind of life. He thinks he hears a clock ticking in the house somewhere, but they do not own any ticking clocks. He gets up in bed, careful not to disturb his wife, who sleeps like a dead Pope. He walks through his house, the one he and his wife bought with the money from their livings. When he thinks of his brother he thinks of him with quotation marks around him. His "brother"... Where has he been? What has he been doing with his life all this time? He wanders to the big globe in his office and spins it to the Pacific Ocean, pinning his fingertip just under Hawaii. He looks at it. He hears a creaking...

Somewhere out in all the dark of the world is your life waiting for you to fall asleep so it can do its work.

Sadness

Have you too been accosted by the sad flashing dogwalker?

He has been lurking in the night, under rainy moons, flashing his entirely flaccid penis to men and women in the neighborhood, all while handling five or six slavering dogs on leashes.

There is no one else to walk the dogs, which is why his awful reign continues.

These are strange and frightening circumstances. He appears so sad, flashing himself. It is as if the object of danger and offense switches from his visible, flaccid penis to his visibly sad face. What person in his position of outrageous power has the right to be so deeply and endlessly sad?

Even in such times, when they are burn-hanging third-borns and malforms in the more superstitious towns, a person like that can sour dreams of a better life.

A Blurry Living That's There

In these memories I can't see a face. It's just a blurry living that's there. Like when you can hear rain but can't see it. And all the foxes wearing pearls of lust come out of the long grass and your headlights pass over them and then it's dark. I think this dream will happen. It will occur. I will have said everything I was meant to say before I die. But that will be the loneliest thing…

Cuckold

I knew this man who left his cuckolding wife for a younger woman who looked like a younger version of his wife. After a brief honeymoon period he then left this younger woman for an even younger woman who looked like an even younger version of his wife. Indeed it could be said she was the "girl version" of his wife. Even while others gave him disapproving looks he then left this "girl version" of his wife for what could only be called the "baby version" of his wife. The man and the "baby version" of his wife lived happily for a couple weeks but the man was in no way fit to cohabitate with any baby, even if it was the "baby version" of his wife. Soon the man left the "baby version" of his wife for another man's penis. The man put his mouth around the other man's penis. When the other man came to the end of his sensation years later, he pulled his penis out of the man's mouth and left, presumably producing some meandering family of his own.

I'm going to read this story again now and see if anything new happens…

I Open I Wince

Two people almost die in a car accident and then they become my parents.

This deadening weight of dread hangs over me my entire life.

Before every door I open I wince.

Falling in love merely feels like falling down, falling through, falling out of the orbit that holds things together.

Success visits me once or twice and it tastes like puckering lemonade, prickling hot sauce, something that puts its feet up on the furniture in the house of my mouth.

I breathe. I close my eyes. I try to sleep. I am very good at none of these things.

Whenever I am able to go home I open the cage I keep the little man in. He shudders out like a pale shadow and offers his hands up to me. I spew into the cupped offering. He moves the cup of his hands to his translucent lips and sips. Clouds move across the moon and become the moon. One of us is satisfied. The other will be soon.

Everybody That I Know In The World

The day before yesterday, a woman mistook me for somebody who is missing.

She ran me down and stopped me and looked at me. Moments before this happened, I heard somebody calling for a Billy, but because my name is not Billy, doesn't even remotely resemble Billy, I did not turn to look. When I realized I was the Billy she was calling for, I became very confused.

I said, "I'm sorry but I'm confused." And she looked at me very deeply, letting some kind of emotion bobble at the surface. Her one hand held my shoulder and her other hand was trying to explain the thing she wanted to say but wasn't saying. Just looking at me very deeply, bobbling. I was very confused.

She said sorry when she realized the mistake. She said, "You're not him." For some reason I said sorry again. She looked so sad I felt as though I had let her down by not being the person she thought I was. She said, "I thought you were Billy, I'm sorry."

Again I said, "I'm sorry I'm not." And her sadness turned to a kind of embarrassment.

She said, "I don't do this all the time; this is the first time I've done this." I just looked at her. She said, "My baby brother, Billy, has been missing for weeks, and for the first time I thought I saw him." She said, "I thought he was you. Or you were him."

Or I was him? I just kept looking at her. People were moving by us but it didn't feel like they were the ones moving. She said, "My parents see him everywhere but I have yet, until just now, to see him in public." She said, "I couldn't tell if it was something wrong with me, that I couldn't see him in public, or if I was just being reasonable and sane because why, if Billy were alive, would he be out walking around and not letting us know he was okay?"

I didn't know what to say. I wasn't Billy so I couldn't answer that question. She seemed to be questioning if she had let reasonability destroy her more passionate senses? I had no answers for her. She walked away and I walked away.

I walked home and sat in my apartment. By this time, I thought I had the answers to her questions. If somebody were there with me I would've felt like saying something about it to them, but in reality wouldn't really say anything. That's always how it is. Even if everybody that I know in the world were sitting right next to me, I can't imagine I'd want to say a single, stupid, little word.

The Mountain

The next year there were many "victories." I walked into the stuttered and half-burnt woods to look for the mountain I had hiked when I was young. It was a small mountain that misted over in the mornings and evenings. From even halfway up you could see the flat expanse of where you could be but weren't. It filled you with big gulping pangs that felt like "life." I've wandered through these woods all my life since. The mists clam up my palms. It's like I can hear the calm, crystal waters being lapped up by a great beast called "The End."

Trust And Understanding

I kneel here licking the doorknob you've just touched to leave the room, but it won't bring you back.

I don't taste your hand there. A hand doesn't linger once it leaves the spot it was just touching. It moves with the rest.

I don't trust fingerprints...

I can't hold them.

Maybe I'm losing my mind...

Maybe I don't understand how anything works at all...

Cole Porter In The Mist

I live every day like I can live it again.

It works like a bruise.

You have to have *jouissance*.

But it's so soft on the senses. What I don't know is like a distant hand covering my face in a photograph…

The problem with every day is we get the chance to repeat love…

No Experience Is Better

What does Helen of Troy have to do with any of this? It is like repeatedly being hit over the head with a broken champagne bottle. All the lights flicker on and off on the beach. Dolphins swim in paradisiacal sludge. Experiences can be so different. It's like being in a different "space." Or "time." But isn't it nice to train a dog "to act?" It begs the question. What will we be reduced to?

Far Too Late

Still so dirty after all these years…

Riding my pale pinto horse into the wrecked pink Porsche of reality…

After a thousand years, after it's far too late, they'd uncover us all in states of self-immolating fashions…

This morning I broke a mirror and behind it I caught a glimpse of Hell…

There were rose-gold candelabras lit by blood on every table…

I imagined someone seated there…

Waiting for hours and hours for someone like me to finally not show.

Cats Cannot Kill Themselves

I was looking for a job and found one as a house cat. My employer is a very large old woman who wears fifty different pearl necklaces around her neck at all times. She has a pair of diamond earrings that dangle from her ears and sometimes I paw at them and she'll say, *No poo-poo.* I walk around the house all day bored but not because there isn't anything to do. I'm just like this. I have a little bell around my neck. It sucks. I find no joy in life. I once tried to hang myself but my employer walked in and said, *No poo-poo, cats cannot kill themselves.* When I get my paycheck every two weeks I walk around all day with nine lives of shame, humiliation, and anger to burn…

These Kinds Of Things

When she wasn't sick, she wanted to be kidnapped. She would ask men to come and kidnap her in the middle of the night and take her to their place, where they'd have sex. She would say *no no, who are you, stop doing this*. She would act like she was trying to work her way out of the rope. She was and she wasn't. It was that kind of thing—the was and wasn't. But now she's dying.

Judy, her mother, called a week and a half ago. She called in the evening. I almost let it ring. Judy said that Celia was sick, had this "thing." Who has what thing? It's a thing, an illness, Judy said. I'm just informing you. I know it would cheer her up to see you. I said okay and that I would go and see her. We hung up. I thought about what kind of thing she had.

Celia doesn't look sick when I finally go to see her a week later. Her hair looks unwashed—that's it. She is asleep when I come in. I don't want to wake her because these kinds of things are so much easier when one person is asleep. I'm looking at her and not looking at her when she wakes up. She says, You look bad. Maybe I've let myself go. I hadn't thought about it. Maybe I'm completely different, and should also be in a hospital bed somewhere. I smile to make myself better-seeming. Celia tries to smile but can't. Two white floaters keep bouncing around in the corner of my eye until I realize they're gulls outside the window.

In the hallway, before the elevators, Judy says: I don't think I have much left in me. She is trying to convey the toll loss has taken on her. She says her husband went with his second heart attack five years ago, and Tommy, the prodigal son, is a meth head who she hasn't seen in eight years. This woman is a clock of melancholy time. Before I get into the elevator that I'm sure will take me to hell, Judy asks me between coughs if I will help with the funeral arrangements.

I was just driving until I didn't feel like driving anymore. So I parked in the parking lot of a park.

I saw a man with a golden retriever. The man was wearing a small cap that barely covered the crown of his skull and I could tell from the short brim and sides of his head that the man was bald. I immediately thought: *cancer.* Everybody has a thing, I thought. Who will take care of the dog when he is dead? Do dogs get cancer? I saw a white van bustle down the road and thought: Is it carrying anyone, roped up and gagged, in the back?

Would Celia want every man who tied her up in the middle of the night and drove her to a strange place to have consensual nonconsensual sex with her at her funeral? She said the most pleasure was the ride in between. *Sometimes.* That feeling of being blindly taken, against one's will, but also *with* one's will, *alongside* one's will. The being taken *is* the will.

Six weeks pass. Celia gets closer and closer but never goes. She seems on the brink every time I see her. The doctor tells Judy the thing is worsening. There's not much more to be done about the thing. Judy nods her head at almost every word, not saying anything, until she looks like a woodpecker just caught in the rote performance of woodpecker. Judy looks at me and says I look like I could use some sleep. But I have been sleeping. I have dreams, erotic ones…legs, folding into and out of nothing…and then too much of…and then…and then I wake up. It's the best sleep of my life. One evening, just the two of us, Celia asks me if I remember that time she asked me to "kidnap" her. I nod my head and check my phone.

I did not understand it back then. I foolishly said yes anyway. Yes yes yes yes. Absolutely. Yes. I was unnerved and also not. Perhaps I was too simple back then to understand what she liked about it. I thought she was leaving me in the weirdest way possible. Like she was trying to *scare* me away, etc. I was young. Younger than she was. It worked. I told myself I would go. I drove by her apartment. Saw her window lit up. The light was the sign. But then I drove away. I didn't even call her. At the time I thought it was because I was too scared, nervous. But now I think it was because I was too embarrassed that I couldn't. Sorry about last night, I texted her the next day. It took her forever to write back. Ages and eons. She wrote, It's okay.

Judy asks me when I'm going to get married. I half-smile and shrug and don't tell her I don't understand what she's just asked me. She says her daughter and I were great for each other and that she wishes we could've worked it out. I feel like refusing this moment between us—this highly emotional, metaphorically clichéd and tender thing between two people losing the same person. But I realize it isn't my moment to refuse. Or it is, and yet I still can't.

The hospital is silent. It's night out and the lights from the dark shape of the other city in the distance twinkle and fade. Judy says it is very beautiful, this view. I look out the window and down below I see the long, big roads that lead to the other city clogged with the headlights and taillights of cars moving back and forth from this city to that one. More taillights than headlights.

The funeral arrangements are placed on hold. Celia is doing better. The doctors say something optimistic. Judy tells me I'm a good luck charm. I'm not sure what she means by this. I don't feel like anything's happened differently by me being here. I tell Celia it's great news. Judy hugs me. I go home and sit in my dark apartment. For a time, I think I can hear my loud embarrassment from years ago, but it ends up just being the evening rain. I turn a light on near the window and wait for the rest of the nothing to happen.

Ambiguous Biography

I am stuck in a motion I can't describe.

I have been rummaging through your stuff and finding myself more and more interested whilst doing it!

It's like we had similar childhoods... We both spoke to strangers!

Many years later, we became those strangers...

We are so very primitive it is almost erotic!

Has something not happened to you too?

The Screaming Speck

A woman pulled a little man out of her vagina. In reality she said, How'd this little man get up in my pussy? The little man, looking up from between the woman's fingers, said, The light! The light! Put me back in! Please! The woman said, I can't possibly do that in good conscience. But why? said the little man. Because, said the woman, it's the law. (There, in fact, was a law that recently passed that indicated men (of any size) shall not be placed in the vagina of any woman, under penalty of "extreme death.") My, said the little man forlornly, much has changed since I've been in there! Yes indeed, the woman said. Then she dropped the little man from between her enormous fingers and watched the screaming speck of him drift like a feather down to the ground until she lost him among the dust and the dirt and the bramble of the magic forest where she had been masturbating.

Made Of Bruises

Let's put it this way: it works. These woods have been haunted since we woke up. Who knows what goes on when we aren't looking? Here's a steak to wipe the blood from your broken nose. We make doppelgängers out of all the injuries we accrue in our lives. Another one of us, made of bruises, lives elsewhere. A blood-soaked shape walks to the beach, buys something in a store, walks into the woods at night…

A Tyranny

A woman dies and gets reborn as a banana.

The banana is not yet ripe—could blend right into the summer grass if it could run away.

So this is what it feels like to live! says the banana. Finally!

But there is no living for the banana. It is a banana now. Do you think we—*we*—would allow something as small and inhuman as a banana to live?

Politeness

I was meeting the man who previously owned the house I now call home. After moving out of the house, almost immediately, his wife died of a brain aneurysm. His children were now grown and at colleges on different coasts. It had been a few years. The reason for the meeting was to give him a box of photos I had found in the bottom of a closet in a room I hardly used in the house. The pictures were mundane but gave off the seductive allure of private lives lived elsewhere.

How was it that all of this had happened without me! How could anything happen without me! I felt the shock of someone realizing they are not the only person alive. A family. People dancing. A dog. Many photos of his children in various stages of growth. I recognized them from when I did a walkthrough of the house before buying it. Buying the house, I had the sensation, born out of jealousy, that I hated this family. They were ugly, dull, and seemed to be already dead. I was buying a home from ghosts—which excited me! It felt like I was going to take their place.

Even though I hated reaching out to people in those days, I found it only right that the man should have these photos of his family. We met at a disgusting café that I despised . He surprisingly looked younger, more alive, interested and interesting: as if losing his family had restored his health. I brought the box of photos, put it on the table. He opened it and began looking.

His initial excitement seemed to turn very quickly into a strange community of features I had never seen on a face before. These are not my photos, he said. Of course they are, I said. No, they are not, he said. These are your children though, I said, picking up a photo of his two children staring coldly into the camera. I've never seen these children before, he said. I mean, they have similar features to mine, he said, but they aren't mine. I thought he was either clearly lying or having a breakdown. These were clearly his dull and ugly children in the photos. But he kept saying no, no they weren't. He ended up refusing to look at them further. He gave me no handshake. He left without paying for the large, gross coffee and slice of pumpkin pie he had ordered. I bit into the pie. It put my stomach in a bad mood, which I reveled in. Leaves fell outside. The box of photos sat there with me. I felt like a man.

The Dildo

My wife and I bought the dildo to make ourselves feel more interesting. We are very mundane people. Our last name might be Smith. It is interesting having a dildo in the house. It isn't too big and it's cerulean, like the room of a newborn who wishes to sleep inside a room that is calm and artistic.

We have never used it. It stays in the drawer in our bedroom. We imagine a nosy houseguest or burglar going through our drawers and finding it and thus imagining us as very interesting, very cool people who have rich private worlds.

It spoke one night to me in a dream, I say to my wife.

Sounds krinky, she says.

It wanted to talk to me about quantum mechanics, I say to my wife.

It's all those science shows you watch, she says.

Then she blows a kiss to me matter-of-factly and goes back to stitching her mitten. She's been working on the mitten for years now, it seems—

certainly since before we were married. I remember it being just thread without a shape then, and now I wonder when she will finish it, and who will wear it, and if it will even fit.

Five Million Beethovens

This is the highway that leads, no matter how dark it is and no matter how few tail lights there are in front of you and no matter which exit you take, to five million Beethovens.

They're out there, not all doing exceptional things.

One is probably making coffee badly... Another is most likely doing sexual intercourse badly... And yes, of course, there is another Beethoven who is doing his taxes badly.

At night, when everyone else goes to sleep, they go to their composition books and pick up their quill pens and begin composing sonatas and symphonies. You can feel them in your blood.

One of the Beethovens says he is composing the color blue, for that is what he heard in the dream with the woman with the tongue like a red scarf.

But all of the Beethovens are deaf. They can only hear in dreams. So they can't hear the other Beethovens doing what they are doing. They think they are the only Beethovens in existence, if they think about being a Beethoven at all. It's strange and sad. If you watch them just before your eyes soften into sleep, they look like Christmas lights on a house where the family dog has just died.

If you come across a Beethoven that can hear, that means you are dreaming…

Openness And Positive Reinforcement

Since she was very little, able to remember her dreams, she wanted to become a car.

Her parents, being of the generation that practiced openness and positive reinforcement, told her that it was a fine dream to have.

But when she grew older, came to that age where the body explores itself through wild desire, and she brought home with her a muffler, her parents were outraged.

Her mother, hands folded in her lap, kept shaking her head silently. No daughter of mine, her father kept saying, no daughter of mine…

It was clear to her then, though unclear in its exact nature, that something for them had changed.

The Greatest

The sun's throat has been slit across the beach. The tide brings it in. You can see everything like this. It's like wearing rose-colored glasses to an execution. People crawl out of these desolated homes near the beach to decide if their life is worth the fright.

I am with you, friend...in these clutching hours of anxiety!

Cheerleaders, in their uniforms of bronze, are cheering my name. Their mothers, who were once cheerleaders too, cheer for me too. They clutch their gold rings and anal pearls. I am not the greatest, but I am like the candle that gives out darkness.

I Have A Friend

I have a friend, Ivan, who is so dumb he just lies around all day among his goats.

What a blissful nincompoop!

He has named one goat Darling. Another goat he has named Rusty. My favorite goat of his is named Appreciation!

It is a goat with a little potbelly, and I love the little guy! I pet him and he does a noise that makes me pinch up inside with happiness. Ah, Appreciation!

I forget how Ivan and I met. He's a...very forgettable person. But his goats are beautiful! They bring me such joy!

Where I live, you see, we cannot have any goats...

The Shadow Knows

I am working and looking at my shadow at the same time. While I work, my shadow works. Even though I cannot see the precise nature of its work, I know that my shadow works when I work. When I am not at work, my shadow is not at work. The precise nature of its leisure is a mystery to me, but I do know that my shadow does not work in the times that I do not work. Which all begs one to ask the question: who is making who work? And how can that despicable scoundrel be stopped?

Deathwatch

The time hurts. I go around and throw the clocks
in the cooking pot. The water boils and evaporates.
And then there's all this blanching on the kitchen
ceiling and walls. When night comes, it all glows.
Just go to bed. Disassemble the senses! It matters
that we don't know! I love that we can't see! But we
go on being haunted by the sound of the ticking. It
even ruins being lazy...

Hospitality

I was the one in charge of the needs of the guests. There were four of them now and one of them was missing a foot.

Where'd your foot go? I said.

The guest shrugged, then said: How am I supposed to know that? I'm just the guest.

I'm very hungry, another guest said. It was the guest with the large belly reading a baby-names book. I'm eating for two, she said. I need to eat, like, an hour ago.

Sorry, I said. I can probably whip up some sandwiches in a sec.

She huffed. We can't all be geniuses, I suppose, she said. Then she said out loud to everybody: Nobody will mind if I play some Mozart? I'm going to play some Mozart. I'm going to play it for the baby because that is a good thing for the baby.

Music that sounded like little naked nymphs gliding through the grass played. For a moment I wished I were the baby before I began feeling sorry for the baby. It still had so much to do yet in life: practically everything... yes, a lot of work ahead for that baby. I felt tired just thinking of all the baby had to accomplish still, so I watched its Mozart-playing mother lumber around the room, semi-gracefully.

Aren't I a great dancer still? she said.

Then she said: I don't mean to be harsh, but you're kind of the worst host.

The other guests agreed by nodding their heads. I felt overworked, drained, bad at everything. A failure, and painfully conscious of it like the spot where I bit my tongue earlier. I felt all these things. Here were these guests and they were not appreciating my efforts! I could not make them happy.

I was trying.

I was.

I was considering making brownies. Everyone loves brownies!

Then: almost at the precipice of it all, before falling over the edge into despair, two more guests showed up, separately, and upon seeing the other said they were sexually attracted to one another. It was love at first sight, they said.

Odd as it sounds: they *emanated* with it. It was as if they were their own brownies.

It was strange to hear the guests declare their love like that, and lovely too. A change occurred in the air of the room. I felt little elevators full of drunk and happy people run up and down my body. It made me feel good I could provide a space for these two people to find each other in. The Mozart played on. The pregnant guest began dancing with the footless guest. I was feeling like I had done a good job… a *decent* job. A job. Having guests means letting them fall in love from time to time. I was immensely happy. The pregnant guest, turning her head to me, kept saying I looked like an idiot, but I beamed from ear to ear and would not stop. I made some brownies and everyone seemed grateful for the company.

Later, I saw everyone to their rooms, where they cozied themselves and rested. I lingered and listened outside the room of the two in-love guests doing in-love things. I tried to imagine what it would be like to be in that room. In the morning I knew I would wake up feeling like I had been dreaming of love.

Inheritance

Cheerleaders, in their uniforms of blood. are cheering my name. I know their moms, who were once cheerleaders too, cheer for me too. They clutch their gold rings and anal pearls. I am like the candle that gives out darkness. Your dad has a tattoo of my face on his ass. I saw it when I smacked it with a fat stack of one-hundred-dollar bills. When he dies, go searching for the money up his ass. I left it in there for you. This is your inheritance.

Something Wrong

There is something wrong about that town. It's not the people or the buildings. Nor is it in the geography of the town. Its wrongness is not in its weather or food. It has nothing to do with its infrastructure or economy. In fact, it is hard to really explain what is wrong with that town. That something is wrong with the town at all is just what we have been told, and that seems well enough for now, and it is always best to leave well enough alone.

No Life To Live

This sadness is like a starved elephant being whipped by a blind clown with scoliosis...

Let us now anticipate and hope!

The moment is at hand when all the toilets in the world begin to shuffle off...away from the daily abuse...to that paradise where all things burdened in one life get rewarded with...no life to live...

Know Thyself!

I feel like I could never do something that needs exactitude and certainty.

I couldn't be a referee, for example.

Uh maybe that was a touchdown…maybe it wasn't though…what, really, is the meaning of the word "touchdown" …who can say what a touchdown even is, is what I would be saying a lot.

The Boy Who Was A Cup

There was a boy who got turned into a cup. A witch did it at the town's request. What they gave the witch in return is still a mystery.

Turning him into a cup was the only way for anybody to get anything out of the boy.

So he lived the rest of his life as a cup.

The unforeseen problem was: the town realized they had to put something into him now before they could get anything out of him.

Will This Ever End

A black velvet night ripples down until I have to turn on all the lights. I pull the ponytail of a lamp and the room ignites. Floating in the one dark corner of the room where there is no lamp is a whiskered face. It watches me and smiles in an animated way, as if something else is living vicariously through what it sees. Who goes there? says I. The whiskered face just smiles. From its dark corner it plops out a glowing orb that bounces onto the floor and rolls to me. What of this? I say. The glowing orb cracks open to reveal a glowing "sad face." The kind you might send on your phone if you were sad or pretending to be sad. What am I to do then with this? I say. But the whiskered face just smiles. It plops out another glowing orb that bounces and rolls to me. It cracks open and reveals another "sad face." The night goes on like this. Will this ever end? I say, holding bundles of "sad faces" in my arms.

I Thought Of The Movie Carrie

I was surprised when she brought him. We hadn't discussed it. We had discussed it as a future thing, but not so soon. I had already begun regressing—expecting a relaxed evening with some moderate discipline.

All night, after the regression but before their coming, I kept having sensations that I had pig blood inside me instead of human blood. I could feel it swirl inside me in unnatural directions.

Then I thought of the movie *Carrie*, which my sister is named after. Everything turns into slow motion at the prom. So slow it is almost like maybe some of the characters are on drugs. Or maybe the camera is on drugs. It is my favorite scene.

We sat on the couch for a bit and talked. She was assuming some kind of authority, slowly, subtly. I was wondering what I was supposed to be doing with my body. My hands especially. Most of the time I put a cup in them but I didn't drink.

After a while she said, bath. But it was so slow it felt like she was saying bath for hours. Is still saying bath. Was always saying bath. I couldn't imagine being alive without her saying bath.

I nodded my head. I have an exceptional bathtub. Big, wide, feet like claws. She filled it up while we—him and I—stood next to each other. She told him to take his clothes off first. For a second or an hour, I wasn't sure which "him" she was telling. Him or the him that was me. We were both him, no matter whose thoughts you were listening to.

He took his clothes off until he no longer had clothes on. He got in the tub because she told him to. Then it was my turn. The water was warm like blood.

We sat in my tub, looking up at her. She looked down at us. She rolled up her sleeves and nursed pitchers of water onto our heads. One head at a time. I could feel something of his on my hand under the water when it was my turn. When she poured the water on his head a feeling of incomprehensible want came over me. I looked up at her.

I thought about what would happen next. If she would let it happen. If she would make it happen. If he knew if she was in the mood to let or make it happen. I had no say in the matter, I decided hours before. I would let anything happen to me. I was in no mood to say what I didn't want.

This Is A Story About Sex Or Power Or Objects

I want objects, when I leave the room, to still hold my spot– outline my absence. I want them to sit there, quietly, in whatever position I leave them, and I want them to think about me. The shoe, on its side, waiting for my foot. The bedside table waiting for some weight to push it back down into the floor. A footstool curled over in worship on the floor for hours…

I want these objects to come alive when I come back. I want them, by elevating above and beyond their normal uses, to show me how much they've missed me.

The Maids

I used to live in a rich man's house with my mother. She was the maid. But there was another maid, too. For some reason the rich man and his wife had different maids. My mother was the rich man's maid. His wife's maid was a woman named Sonya. She didn't have children, but she did have a baby bear cub she kept on a chain in her room. I wasn't allowed in her room. Every Saturday night the rich man and his wife would have both of their maids fight in front of the gold-cherubic fireplace. They would provide both maids with weapons and tell them to fight. Sonya was a very good fighter. I remember her shoulders—they were very big. Her muscular thighs. Her hands were excellent. I always felt bad for my mother. She sometimes won, but never really won even when she did. When I grew up and left the house for university, my mother stayed behind, and I never saw her again. I see Sonya everywhere.

Just Die

A shoe told me to die once. It was actually an ad for the shoe. It said, "Just die." But this was in the days of me not being able to read. I now know the shoe on the ad was telling me to "just do it." Which, to me, is more vexing, less concrete, and completely vague...

The Humongous Man Of Her Dreams

On the TV show is a fat man–humongous– and all
of a sudden she says she wants a fat man.

I'm a fat man, I say to her.

No, she says. Not enough.

I can be fatter! I say. I swear! Don't do this to me!

I can't believe I'm begging now. In a matter
of seconds my life became something else: all
the comfort slipped out. One moment we were
watching tv and the next moment I'm palpitating
with anxiety. I don't want to be left for a humongous
man! But a humongous man is what she wants.
When she gets an idea it, almost without fail,
becomes reality.

For days we cruise around public places—malls,
restaurants, men's big and tall shops, etc.—looking
for the humongous man of her dreams.

Yes, of course, I could just walk away. You're
saying to yourself: just walk away, you not-fat-
enough pathetic fool. She doesn't love you! So why
stay? Why help her look for your replacement?

I don't want to.

If I had a photo for every day of my life I did the thing that was good for me, I'd have very few photos. None maybe. Maybe one.

Oh, look at *him*, she says to me from behind her disguise of big black sunglasses and black mustache. He's humongous, she says with wonder, with hope.

I look at this enviable man. He walks strangely, as if he couldn't walk any other way. As if he were constantly hula hooping a ghostly hula hoop around his waist. Where his head meets his shoulders looks like an octopus trying to squeeze itself messily into the center of him. His belly, if it is a belly anymore and not another entity entirely, is massive, barely able to be shirted. This man is goddamn beautiful!

She stares at him from behind her sinister disguise, almost in agony of desire, tormented by that special friction of lust and love. I stare at her staring at him and can barely control myself, this feeling of too much to name, too much to die of. We stay like that, neither of us making a move, not ready yet, until her humongous man disappears into his life, happily unaware how close he was to being loved.

A Mood That It Happened

I had a dream I died. But it wasn't in the usual way. I died in the dream like how a person forgets what they dreamt the night before. As if it actually happened but didn't. Only in a feeling. A mood that it happened. But you can't quite slip back into that mood. And so the feeling just hangs there on the side of things like a velvet night waiting to be pulled in on a hook to replace daytime. And you just lie on your bed naked, eating, and liking things. And it's not like I was frightened by the death that happened to me. I woke up like the melodious reverb of a harp tuned to another life. Like I wasn't real and didn't have authority over anything but didn't have to be and didn't have to. And all the flowers popping out for spring had blood already sprayed on them. But nobody took this as an omen.

Sex Is Not A Season

In my youth I was a manic pixie dream girl. But now I'm a 29 year-old man who is very tired.

The season doesn't matter. Fall, summer, spring, whatever others there are...

Often I go to the park. I see couples walking in the park, their hands together, mouths directed at each other, and I run up to them and interrogate them.

What do you think you're doing? I will ask. *What do you know? How long have you known? Who do you work for?*

One time a boyfriend of a woman answered in a very serious voice: Pfizer.

Work Hard, Achieve, Get Married

When I was a teenager, my friends and I drunkenly killed a man walking on the side of the road. Hit him with the car very fast. We dumped his body in the nearby ocean. We made a pact of silence. Take it to the grave. Blood oath. Etcetera.

Twenty years later here we are, looking out windows of high buildings, coming home to families, sleeping well at night, we are so very successful. Nobody has come for us. Nobody will come.

If we look over our shoulders it is because someone has just tapped us there, usually to hand us back a dollar bill we've dropped or to shake our hand.

Work hard, achieve, get married, buy a house, make it a home.

The Second Executioner

John the Baptist was decapitated by a man who had a foot fetish.

The man was the second executioner in the court of Herod Antipas. The first executioner had off the day John the Baptist was to be executed.

The second executioner—whose name translated from the Galilean means "cedar rot"—beheaded John the Baptist in the customary manner but fumbled the head onto the silver platter. The highly unusual request was what caused the fumbling. The second executioner found the thought of a severed head on a silver platter outrageous! But he couldn't deny the passion in it.

He looked at the head on the silver platter. He no longer thought of the head as "John the Baptist," or even "John the Baptist's head." It was now just the head. The head's mouth was open. The second executioner took his forefinger and thumb and pinched together the lips of the head.

Later, the head was presented to Herod's court. Wine was served in fluted goblets. Roasted goat, on a bed of apricots, was the main course. The second executioner thought the spectacle gauche, so he enjoyed just three figs and left.

When the second executioner returned home, he laid down under the feet of his second wife. Having no interest in what her husband did for a living, the second executioner's wife did not ask him how his day was. She put her lips together and blew out the candle on the table and drew with her finger in the curls of smoke. *Another day*, she said haughtily. She dangled each foot above him, dipping a toe every now and then into the wet openness of his mouth.

Crawl On Me

A lot of times, after having disgusting sex at her slow nephew's cabin, we'd just get very sick of each other and begin volleying hurt back and forth.

Don't call my nephew slow, she'd say.

I have a cousin who's slow, I'd say. It's okay.

My nephew's not slow though, she'd say.

Have you met him? I'd say.

She'd put her silver hair up, spit in my shoe. I'd tell her not to do that. Oh what are you going to do, she'd say. And I wouldn't do anything.

Why am I thinking of this now?

I think it's because I was feeling very bored yesterday: a deep, gnawing kind of boredom that begins to change the community of blood inside me. So bored I was, in fact, that I had raced in my car away from my big house to the nearest grocery store. I thought it was going to be like the old days. I'd pick up an older lady in the bakery section, whisk her away, pack of donuts hitting the floor, and let her do disgusting things to me, and vice versa. She'd have a slow nephew, too, and we'd go to her slow nephew's cabin and not have children that looked like us.

Nothing happened though. The grocery store was practically empty. A couple of construction workers waited for meat at the deli. A little boy on tiny crutches, with his average-looking mom, was walking down an aisle. Not one older vixen! Outside, an ugly as hell employee on his smoke break asked me if I wanted to get high. I hated his stupid fucking dumb as shit red hair. I told him that, too. I was looking for something to happen. He punched me in the face—he was strong!

I stayed down on the ground for a little bit: desperately hoping somebody—anybody—might crawl on me and do sexual things to me while I lay there. Soon though the manager of the grocery store came out and said get. Just kick me a little, I said. Go, he said. Just spit on me and give me one kick! I pleaded. Get, freak, he said, or I'm calling the cops. I got up, unsatisfied, and left.

On my way home—after wondering if I might be the exotic topic of dinner conversation later in the grocery store manager's home; his wife and children all going to bed with steamy, misty thoughts of me in their boring heads—I ended up with only my memories of when getting hurt was fun. I was older now, too. I was naïve to think there'd always be a person willing to hurt and be hurt as much as myself. When I was young, I had an image of a disembodied mirror moving through life with me. It was its own entity, distinct from myself. We'd hold hands, and be best friends, and in the end get married. But there are no mirrors out there. When I look into people's faces I—like a vampire—don't see anything of me there!

I started to laugh! Ha ha ha! I was in a BMW, unlucky as fuck, lights all turning on around me in the evening, not caring at all that I had somehow let myself—finally, after so many years—become myself.

Fairytale That Has Stopped Working

A handsome man walked into his reflection in a mirror. On the other side he came out as a princess. The princess kissed a frog and turned into a fly. The frog ate the fly and turned into a dildo. Moss grew over the dildo and turned it into a tree. Lightning struck the tree and turned it into a magic acorn. A mischievous boy took the magic acorn and ate it. The acorn grew into a tower in the boy's belly. The tower ripped through and out of the boy's belly and grew so tall it disappeared into the clouds. A single crane flying west crashed into the tower, splitting it in two and sending the pieces toppling to the ground, creating two women. The two women looked at each other, each of them thinking they were looking into a mirror. They tried to walk away in opposite directions but they couldn't. They shared the same hair.

Such

I wonder where the dog goes at night, after we've all fallen asleep. He always comes back in the morning very satisfied. The look on his face is so happy and content I want to eat it in my cereal.

Nice night out? I ask him.

Oh you know, he says.

He's such a coy motherfucker. I love him. He's such a good boy.

King of Thrills

You dive into the crystal lake and I sit on the shore playing with your clothes you left in a pile. I think: *These are your clothes that you are no longer wearing.* And that puts me in a certain kind of mood. This is the lake a little boy drowned in years ago. Here, everything is like something else. Your bare feet stick up out of the water. Red toenails on them. And behind them, a sunset in the distance like a garland of fire. I watch while I hold a pair of powder blue panties like a crown I want to place atop my head. Every time you disappear under the water, I think I've seen the last of you, and that thrills me, but then when I see you again, that thrills me even more. And as the dark settles in around the lake, I think: *I am the King of Thrills, and all of this is mine.*

This Is A Story About Food Or Jealousy

In a diner at night, the man with the hat was eating the food brought to him by the waitress.

He didn't think much of the food at first— generously heaping it into his mouth—until he noticed this was not what he had ordered…

He first noticed by taste, then by sight, not what it was but that it was different than what he had ordered.

When he called the waitress over and asked her what this food was, she just laughed… Out of a deep void from within she laughed. She began gushing dark liquid from her mouth. She went and served another table in this state…

The man with the hat felt a pulsing urge to finish the food now. Something enlivened his veins: he could feel them all making up the shape of him. He put his face into the food and consumed it. He ate and ate until he felt a dark heartbeat replace whatever had been there.

Beached

Science can't teach me what others don't understand…

Eye to eye, the view is so different.

A drop of ejaculation or a milky sunset?

Happiness in the form of desired punishment?

Saying *daddy, daddy, daddy* without getting any reaction is a form of prayer for some people.

The beach turns out to be a beached whale…

Let's live here, says the tribe of corporate board members washing ashore in a wave of blood.

The Fire Eater

It was in Ohio, where I was seeing the fire eater for some time. Take away the fire eating and he was not a particularly interesting man. He thought he was more interesting than he really was. He would become angry that I sometimes didn't talk. He'd come home, his lips greasy and blue, and start berating me about why I was so antisocial . I'd say, I'm not antisocial, and then I'd say, some people would call fire-eating anti-social. He'd stare at me and call me anti-social and then go off about all the ways I was anti-social, which, ultimately, seemed to validate his uninteresting personality. He couldn't believe a woman would want to be alone or not in the mood to talk to him. He had so many notions in his head that he had received from clichéd or rote sources that he figured he knew the world top to bottom. And his fire eating, the profession and "art" he said he so carefully chose, was his reaction to this world he was trying to rebel against. In bed, his head falling asleep on the pillow, he always called himself subversive. My insistent calm in the face of his rage and narcissism only frustrated him and so he would tie me up and leave me in the dark bedroom. It was peaceful in those bonds and I remember those periods of dark, silent reflection with a familiar calm. From my spot in that darkness I'd hear him fumbling around in the kitchen in the next room, uninterestingly, predictably: a fork scraping on a plate, a bottle being plopped down on the table, the television being clicked on and humming to life, etc. After a while he'd come in and sit down next to me on the bed and tell me how sorry he was for doing this, for tying me up like that, and he'd bawl and wail, and I'd have to say *there there* and suffer holding him like he was my own birthed failure, my own little boy with bad and hot breath, after which I'd feel depleted and snuffed out, like a still-smoking candle...

I have known many freaks in my life, flitting from city to city as I have for various reasons (both geographical and temperamental), but he is one of the ones I enjoy remembering instead of still knowing.

Dream Of A Silent Night

The shortest day of the year happens and then the longest night and then the longest day. You put on stockings for the evening. Your hand twitches because it misses something. Someone calls and breathes into your year. Your ear. I meant to write "your ear." It doesn't matter. You can't even hear me...

Fly That Can't Fly

Once, I was a baby brought forcibly into the world.

Now I am just a great echoing scream of silence that has come out of a mother.

I walk around like a fly that can't fly anymore. Sometimes I bump into another silence.

Sometimes I can't understand why death has to be permanent…

I am in love with being able to take back the hardest of decisions…

My mother, from the tiny jar she is kept in, says something about being lucky.

Married For Christmas

She met him "online."

It had been a while since she had been "intimate." He said he worked at a "law firm." She liked how he said certain "words." Their third date they had "ice cream." They met "families." They "said" I love you.

May I use your yard to burn some "things?" he asked her one day.

She, being in "love," said: Yes please.

The next day he came over to her place and built a large fire pit in the middle of her yard. She thought this was "odd," but thought he must really need this.

She watched him throw many "things" into the fire. The fire got big. One "thing" she saw him throw in the fire was a large and heavy trash bag. He had to heave it into the fire.

What are these "things?" she asked him.

These are "nothing," he said. I'm a "new" "man."

She could feel the fire get hotter. I love "you," he said. Will you "marry" me?

Even after the fire died down and she could see the scorched bits of bones in the pit in her yard, she said, "Yes," but she couldn't tell if it was because she felt a certain "way" or if she had completely misspoken.

Egresses

The bitten peach of early morning comes back.
    Like an arm reaching.
    Somehow it keeps coming up, then going away.
    I waste half my days of summer thinking of
whose dreams I've been invading at night.

One Nude

You send a nude to your ex-boyfriend, the one who is…well, he's indistinguishable in the sea of former failures, so best not to wrack our brains trying to make him interesting or worth a third-party's time! But you send the nude because it is revenge. You know the value of a nude is in "future possibilities." But for him, there are no "future possibilities." And even a nude loses potency after so long. There are Invisible Hands at work! There is only so much that can be done with one nude. After a while it is just an unclothed body that has been wasted by Capitalism. See? Go underground, friend, into the moist darkness and see all of us, waiting for nothing, who were once just nudes.

A Very Scary Story

Bob woke up with a bloody tooth in his mouth. Bob felt it scraping up against his own teeth and spit it out onto his bed. He felt around inside his mouth to make sure it wasn't his. He had all of his teeth. He looked at the bloody tooth on the covers in front of him. It was long and had stringy viscera hanging out of one end. Bob could taste a tangy metallic flavor in his mouth. This had not been his year. Earlier, during spring, his wife had been violently murdered by a crazy ex-lover of hers. His attentions at work were divided and scattered…he couldn't seem to handle his accounts, and he was summarily let go soon thereafter.

Do your job! Work well! Be a helpful and considerate employee or bad things will befall you!

Tenderness

I have a friend who is nagged by this memory of a very indecent Garfield comic strip. He says it is actually quite sexy, but incredibly perverse, and not just because it involves an anthropomorphic cat and meatloaf. He says it haunts him nightly. He's been losing sleep over it. He can see the strip clear as day in his head, but has yet to find it in real life. He doesn't even like Garfield that much, and never has, so he knows it is not a thing he has purely invented. He knows he must have seen it somewhere, and when he did see it, he thought: Gosh, that's perverse. That's perverse for a kid's comic, he thought. He tries to explain the comic strip but can't. He sees it in his head but can't explain it out loud, out of his mouth. It doesn't come out. He worries that this is either because (A) he has secretly invented the sexy Garfield comic strip in the fabric of his own mind, or (B) he has a brain tumor and/or early onset dementia. Even with these options very much at play as objective realities, he adamantly denies inventing the Garfield comic strip. He says it exists. He talks and talks about it as if it exists.

I let him talk about it. I don't believe him, but I think it's a necessary part of being a friend sometimes to let them live in their delusions. I call that tenderness.

John Jerks Jon

John jerks Jon off in the bathroom while music of the moment plays…

Sam says to the bartender, "I am so existential right now."

A drink gets poured that will sit in a gold and mirrored room and grow warm…

Brinkley asks Kimber if metallic is in right now while Xao-Tim explains to both of them his idea for an art piece that is just an empty cage called "Tiger."

"I have just taken ecstasy," says Coral and Gabe at the same time in different black velvet rooms.

My Curse

I dress up like a teenager and go back to high school to understand what it's like to be held responsible for everything that's happened and will happen...

In my proud mink I roll up in my wheels into the talking parking lot!

I make friends with everyone: my curse...

Instead of listening to what I have to say, they all kiss each other's assholes unabashedly and say they want to save something in the near future...

What can I hate now that my perfect sensibilities have been tainted by all this juvenile lovey-doveyness?

The Gerbil Finds You

Sixty-three years later, the lost gerbil finds you again on the sidewalk. It has rheumatism and walks with a cane now.

You adjust your bifocals on your nose to see clearer this vision from your youth.

Herbert! My god, I've missed you, you say when you recognize him.

Yes, yes, Herbert says.

We all thought you died, you say. One day you were just gone and we thought you died.

Yes, yes, Herbert says. I did not.

What happened to you?

Herbert leans on his little cane, bows his little gray head, and says: I just had to get out of that house...away from that life...I just had to leave...

You nod and say, Yes, I understand.

A moment of intense, quiet swelling happens between the two of you.

You hunch over, lean into it.

Herbert drops to his little knees and says, But oh how I miss those days in that house now. Oh how I miss them!

Clean

I am taking off my underwear and holding them
in my hands now because you told me to. I am
placing my underwear in my mouth so that a
little bit of them sticks out now. I am getting on
my hands and knees and placing my face down
on the hardwood floor so that the little part of my
underwear that is sticking out is also touching the
floor. I am cleaning the floor you are peeing on
now with the little part of my underwear and my
eyebrows and some of my hair. I can feel some of
the pee drip onto my back, which is bared, while
I move my face around the hardwood floor. I am
lifting my head up now because you told me to and
then you spit right in the middle of my face, which
is already wet, so I'm only feeling the force of the
impact when it hits the bridge of my nose and the
lower part of my left eye. I am lowering my head
and going back to cleaning the floor because you
say to. I am continuing to move my face around
on the hardwood floor until you say otherwise,

and it seems like a very long time you do not say otherwise because my head keeps moving back and forth on the hardwood floor, with the little part of my underwear sticking out of my mouth, soaking up the pee that you have made there. Later, after the hardwood floor is clean, I am remembering the one thought I had during the whole scene, because it is indeed the only single thought I had during the whole scene, which branched into many single thoughts, perhaps from the same single tree of thought, and it is: *I am cleaning now the mess I myself have made, I made this mess myself and now I am cleaning it, This mess I made myself is what I must clean right now, Now I myself am cleaning a mess I myself made, This is a mess I made myself and now I must clean it.*

Moral Of The Story Told In That Village During
Happy Times

When having a baby, if you must have a baby, it is best to remember, while looking down at it in its first wet, loud moments of being alive, that everything that happens to people will eventually, one day, happen to your baby.

The Black Jeweled Box Of Clarity

We gulp through all this. It helps but shouldn't. It makes total sense. It's easy to have answers. Having questions is the hard part. Our angels come down like tormented weather. Isn't it supposed to be warm now? We can open the black jeweled box of clarity, but we can't understand how to use what's in it. I'm infected by this jezebel spirit. I'm dancing on the dead dreams of "the System." I have a heart that is a cup runnething over with newish mystery!

A Tiny Person

Imagine a tiny person inside you who controls everything.

They live either in one of your teeth or in a nipple.

Imagine all they want is pain. That is it. Imagine that. Imagine how much worse it could be.

Dolphins

It is cool to be unmotivated and dead. Do what I do. Be on the beach in sunglasses while it pours and pours. It's amazing how much of the ocean is made up of just being looked at. How does something survive in that existence? Where do the dolphins go? It is time to convey how much the prison industrial complex is ruining how we give and receive love. It is like "the death of the author" floating headless around your bed while you sleep. Imagine this kind of "synergy": on one beach is the act of erasure going out with the tide while on another, miles and miles away, washing ashore in a wave of blood is its effect.

The Rabbit

The day is so hot it makes even the black cat on the fence go wavy. The boy and his father are cleaning up in the other yard. It sounds like the yard is in post-winter shambles… The pond is back to moving now. Stray limbs of insects, dead leaves, and bodies of dirt have collected at the edges of the pond, making it dirtier than it will be in a couple weeks. The father says the pond looks better than last season. There are two pieces of wood. They are large enough to be the trunks of trees. They have jagged edges carved into them. The father was carving them to be chairs. They were left unfinished. Autumn came, among other things in that house. The boy helps the father move the first piece of wood. Beneath the wood, the grass is gone except for a few strands of yellowed weeds. Pale worms writhe away from the sunlight. A beetle the boy thinks looks ancient slowly curls itself into the dirt. Have to get some seed, the father says. They take the first piece of wood and hurl it into the woods and then, taking long breaths, go to the second piece of wood. Under the second piece of wood, they find the same: grass gone, yellowed, sickly colored, worms crawling back into the cold earth. Only this time something else is there. It is gray and flattened but they both know it is the body of a dead rabbit. It is lying on its side, as if sleeping. The boy looks at it. He tries to make out if it is still breathing. It is so flat. I can't believe that's a rabbit, says the boy. The father does not say anything. He goes away and then comes back, whooshing open a trash bag. The boy uses a rusty shovel to wake the rabbit from the ground. It does not move and the body is hard, stiff, both alive and not. The father makes a down-and-up gesture with his thumb. The boy just stares at the rabbit. He does not move. Here, the father says, give me that. He takes the shovel in his right hand and carefully lifts the rabbit into the trash bag in his left hand. He puts the trash bag into the trash can. Do not tell your sister, says the father.

Instruments of Doom

The instrument of our eventual doom only plays three notes. And only at night. But they are notes that can only be played by a person who has experienced a certain amount of...*experience*. Nobody has experienced that amount though! And even if they did, there is nobody who knows what the three notes are, so this very experienced person would just be endlessly trying three note combinations. Almost forever. Which would end up creating some very lovely melodies. Enough of them to live out the rest of our lives to.

The Hand Dances

The hands started coming in late summer. It was August. Everything was reaching a point of no return, slipping into fast warm numbness.

We were standing on Mrs. Pagaldy's porch. Mrs. Pagaldy was an old woman but now she was dressing better. You could tell she was paying closer attention to what she looked like, but also that it didn't take so much effort to look that way. I noticed.

Mum was asking about the hand. The Pagaldys' hand arrived the previous Friday, confirming they were one of the poor.

That's who the hands found: the poor, the downtrodden, the weak.

At school the gossip would trickle down from our parents and into our mouths. Those kids whose homes had been found by hands were ridiculed and picked on. It was easy. We didn't think about it.

It's been amazing! said Mrs. Pagaldy on her porch. It's crazy, but I feel frisky.

Frisky? said Mum.

Mrs. Pagaldy didn't say anything. She just smiled and when she smiled it changed her face. I didn't understand it, but couldn't stop looking at it.

Mum wasn't so taken. She stanched her face, said: Well we have to get going.

You don't wanna come in and see it? asked Mrs. Pagaldy.

No no, said Mum. We must be going.

Walking back home, I turned and looked back on Mrs. Pagaldy as she closed her door, still smiling, a little movement in her hips. I felt sorry for her and Mr. Pagaldy and Violet, their daughter who got picked on in school. I could feel a fuzziness around my heart, which I took to understand as a kind of acknowledgment of how pathetic they were—how they needed a hand—and how I wasn't sure I could do anything about it.

When we got home Mum didn't say anything when Dad asked what it looked like. He was on his back, outstretched; he looked like a dead man.

My little brother, Andy, was near him on the floor, saying something into a broken doll's ear.

They're happy, Mum said after a long silence that felt like the time it takes for fruit to rot.

That's good to hear, said Dad. He was staring up at the ceiling.

Andy whispered into the doll and then pounded his fist into the carpet. He was my little brother but I never talked to him. He was raccoonish, wordless, strange. I imagined him as a version of me that had stopped growing, but that was also somehow normal. He was normal because he was part of me, which didn't mean I wasn't ashamed of him sometimes.

There were parts of my home life, my family notwithstanding, that I fantasized about changing. I loved them but there was a fierce urge to change them, too. I'd fall asleep and dreams would spill out in the darkness of a future life that felt easier, but in a vaguer sense than I could ever describe.

I never knew we were poor until the hand came. It was on a luminous October morning, after breakfast, that it appeared. It stood on our porch, near our weeping bench swing, on pollen-dappled fingers.

I looked at Mum. She had a face of someone who was excited but also deeply sheepish about being excited. She wouldn't look at me. I expected more out of her face—a look of profound mortification, or anything close. But no. She said to the hand: Come in, come in!

It did its own tiny version of the Charleston into our home.

Andy was sprawled on the kitchen floor, punching blocks in drool-stained corduroys when he saw it. It bounced in and he squealed with joy. As if understanding it perfectly, he pointed at the hand and watched without fuss. He had not squealed that way since finding a dead bird in the backyard a year before, and even then we couldn't tell if it was in curious joy or frightened dread. This was unmistakable though. The squeal translated into enchantment.

Dad on his back turned his head and watched as the hand did an impish jig for him. Dad smiled. Mum came over, sat, leaned over Dad to share in the moment with him. He looked up at her and she looked down at him. The hand danced on.

As if in spotlight, it performed a swan-like ballet, tiptoeing in and out of the kitchen and into the living room. Only the tips of its fingers getting dirty on our unclean floors.

I stood with my back to the wall. I could almost feel the shadow on it there. A hotness deep in my face seemed to burn.

Mum asked me if I would like to call Kathy and invite her over to see, but I said no I would not.

Later, I fled to the backyard to get away. I could hear them, my family, laugh inside as the hand danced still. Outside, the stars looked like stars and the air was crisp, I remember. Someone was burning wood and something inside me curled

145

up. The demented banjo player who haunted the neighborhood streets at dusk played a twangy, regretting song I can still remember in my bones.

I kept the secret of the hand from friends as best I could. But eventually it got out. It was hard to keep the hands a secret. Parents would talk to each other. Word got around. It was my last year of school, I had a part-time job, I was ready to be free of it all. I was having terrible dreams of being squeezed by what I thought to be huge hands made of night. At school, the guys started acting stranger. As if they wanted to say something but couldn't or wouldn't. It was almost worse than just saying it. Everything was on the side, slanted, sliding.

One night at home I happened upon the hand doing a lively tap in the kitchen for Andy, who clapped like a deranged seal. The hand noticed me, greeted me with a swift, rhythmic tapping and bow. It sounded like the soft cracking of knuckles. Scram, handjob, I said. It pirouetted out of the room. Its abrupt leaving made Andy wail but not the wailing of a small child—it was deeper, more somber. Shut up, I said to him when I couldn't take it anymore.

At dinner one night, I said out loud so that the hand would hear: This is the stupidest thing in the world. The hand did hear. It had been doing a kind of belly dance in the corner of the room as we ate, but now its thumb hung at its side forlornly. It stopped its belly dance and waltzed sadly with an invisible partner out of the room. I didn't feel bad.

Mum asked me to apologize but I said I would not. Dad began to say something from his spot on the floor but I didn't hear it. Neither him nor Mum were in any shape to combat or assuage how I was feeling. Not only were they under the happy spell of the hand, but they both were quickly falling apart. I couldn't remember the last time I saw Dad upright. His body was turning into a letter from a dead language. Mum was not only going deaf but was beginning to slowly crumble away upstairs. She was inching down the staircase that would take her, dreamlike, to a place she couldn't call us from until she finally died, unable to recognize any of us.

It seemed like all of us were moving in vastly opposite directions very fast in our little home. We didn't know it then, but those were the last of the really fine years.

I have this later memory of Dad, almost upright, propped against Mum, on such blue-sweetened nights, under stars bright as crystal, singing songs he had sung when he was younger. It was like he was soothing the spirit of the air with that cracked voice of his. I remember listening to it and feeling that sensation of dripping inside me. All of this under a moon with a mustache made by a passing bat, bird, or plane headed someplace else.

That fall, for a few evenings a week plus the weekends, I would work at Roy Farmer's pumpkin patch. I was in charge of the pumpkins.

Roy always seemed to be wearing sequins somewhere, and his hats looked like pet birds of royalty atop his head. In all the years I knew him, he was a kind and generous man. He said taking care of pumpkins is like taking care of babies. I don't have one of those, I said. That's for the best right now, I'd say, said Roy.

Still, after a week of "pumpkin-rearing" he told me I was keen for this line of work. I had some kind of knack for it. Which made me feel good, like I was another person.

And I did love those pumpkins like they were my own.

In that savage green moss I'd sit and tend to them. I'd ward off the garden pests, and scrub them when they'd get tagged by local teens. It was never anything awful—just the usual harmless and secret slang between voices in the night or some cosmic retort to the shit-raining universe. Nothing I couldn't take care of. With gentle hands I'd scrub them clean. Roy made it clear to never throw any of them away. They could always be rehabilitated, he said. So I scrubbed and scrubbed. Sometimes until my hands were numb.

All the while, at home, I knew Mum and Dad and Andy were cozy, being entertained by the dancing hand.

I'd come home in the dark and Mum would be the only one still up, waiting for me. She'd creak alive and wrap me in her arms and say: We really missed you tonight…

My friend Kathy, who I was keen on and she on me, said I was being rough on the hand, and on everybody really.

It's just a hand, she said.

It's not just a hand, I said. It's what it means.

You're thinking too much about it, Kathy said.

You don't have a hand, I said, so you can't tell me.

Kathy looked at me. Her eyes were big and as always they worked themselves into me—making me feel this odd, reshaped kind of feeling. As if I were a room that had been furnitured by a stranger with only my best interests in mind. I was less scattered, warmer.

I just don't understand it, I said.

You don't have to, she said. Your family likes it. It makes them happy.

I thought about Kathy's answer. It was a good one. I couldn't argue with it. I didn't want to.

Do you want to make out? I asked Kathy.

Not right now, she said.

Okay, I said.

She touched my hand with her hand, which was attached to an arm, an arm that was attached to a whole body. And we've lived like this for centuries…

We carved a pumpkin I brought from Roy's patch.

I can still remember that face but I can't describe it.

Later I went back to the pumpkin patch and thought about what Kathy had to say. I did not want to go home just yet. I sat amongst the quiet, unnatural babies. My hands glided over them and I felt them. I rubbed my hands together and felt them still.

A mist fell down on us from the lateness of the pink autumn sky and I thought of home.

The home was ours and always would be: the place we would come back to after being out in the world. Where I went after caring for those glorious pumpkins, after visiting with Kathy, and so on. I stood outside and looked at it. Inside, the hand was doing its somersaults, its tumbles, its ballet and swings. Without seeing them, I could see my family's mouths, one by one, widen and release laughter from out of the dark tunnels their bodies were made of. They go through my head like voices composed of images: Mum, trying to exert the last of her grace and dignity by sitting straight and proper on the couch... Dad, with a howling Andy leaning on his shoulder, painless and happy... And somehow me there too, again. A white moon broke in through the window and lit us up and we glowed like fish in an aquarium. The hand, from nowhere, whom we had welcomed into our home, flipped backward and did a perfect split. We applauded. It spun then, fast and fast and faster, on one finger, moving time as it did.

I think of it and think of it these days as if it is a memory I made up or dreamt.

Have you ever seen a hand dance?

It really is a happy, happy sight.

I am a long way away from being home in that house but can summon it as easily as casting the shadow of my hand on the bedroom wall at night. The hand is bigger than back then, but it dances and dances still—until I finally fall asleep.

The stories of this book silently collected themselves together over several years under the encouragement and love of my family—Mom, Dad, Carrie, and Andy. Thank you.

Thank you, Cary. For P["["".

Thank you to the Bucks County Free Library, Cornell University's MFA program, and the United States Postal Service.

And infinite thanks to Kevin Sampsell and to Emma Alden.

Shane Kowalski lives in Pennsylvania. He works for the United States Postal Service.

CPSIA information can be obtained
at www.ICGtesting.com
Printed in the USA
BVHW032313221222
654897BV00003B/129